LARK
HAS THE SHIVERS

NATASHA DEEN

Illustrated by MARCUS CUTLER

orca Echoes

ORCA BOOK PUBLISHERS

For Mom and Dad

Text copyright © Natasha Deen 2022
Illustrations copyright © Marcus Cutler 2022

Published in Canada and the United States in 2022 by Orca Book Publishers.
orcabook.com

Library and Archives Canada Cataloguing in Publication
Title: Lark has the shivers / Natasha Deen ; illustrated by Marcus Cutler.
Names: Deen, Natasha, author. | Cutler, Marcus, 1978- illustrator.
Series: Orca echoes.
Description: Series statement: Orca echoes.
Identifiers: Canadiana (print) 20210167165 | Canadiana (ebook) 20210167181 |
ISBN 9781459826052 (softcover) | ISBN 9781459826069 (PDF) | ISBN 9781459826076 (EPUB)
Classification: LCC PS8607.E444 L365 2022 | DDC jc813/.6—dc23

Library of Congress Control Number: 2021934077

Summary: In this illustrated early chapter book, Lark and Connor
are asked to solve two mysteries in one day! When pets go missing
from the local fair and Sophie's house appears to be haunted, the
Ba twins have only a little time to figure out a lot of problems.

Orca Book Publishers is committed to reducing the consumption
of nonrenewable resources in the making of our books. We make
every effort to use materials that support a sustainable future.

Orca Book Publishers gratefully acknowledges the support for its publishing
programs provided by the following agencies: the Government of Canada,
the Canada Council for the Arts and the Province of British Columbia
through the BC Arts Council and the Book Publishing Tax Credit.

Cover artwork and interior illustrations by Marcus Cutler
Author photo by Curtis Comeau

Printed and bound in Canada.

25 24 23 22 • 1 2 3 4

Chapter One

My name is Lark Ba, and I have the eye of the tiger. Well, not really. That would be mean. Tigers need their eyes. *Eye of the tiger* means you have a winner's attitude. I have a winner's attitude. So does Max, our family dog. The annual pet show is tomorrow, and we've been practicing hard.

At this event every pet gets a chance to show off their talent. That's the ~~tuffest~~ ~~touphest~~ toughest part, because it's hard to pick just one! Max can sit and stay. He knows how to shake paws, and he knows lots of words, including *cookie*, *treat*, *dinner* and *lunch*. Plus, he's a very sweet dog, and I think that's the best kind of talent.

This year I wanted to teach Max a special trick. Er, *Connor* and I wanted to teach Max a special trick. Connor is my *little* brother, but he'd get grumpy if he heard me say that.

For the pet show, Connor and I have taught Max how to do math! Dogs know how to count. I know this because I read it in a book I borrowed from the library. Here is how we do our neat trick.

One of us asks Max a question like, "What's two plus two?"

The word *plus* is our cue word. That means when Max hears it, he springs into action. He barks. When he gets to the correct number, Connor winks at him. That is Max's cue to stop barking. Then I dance around to really let Max know to stop barking. Our trick is great, but we aren't perfect. Sometimes Max gets really excited because he loves to bark, so it is hard to get him to stop.

"Lark." Connor came into the family room. He rubbed his eyes. "What are you doing up?"

"I woke up early to practice with Max for the show."

"It's too early," said Connor. "You're supposed to be sleeping."

"It's nine o'clock."

He shook his head. "No, it's only six."

Oops. I have dyslexia, which means I sometimes mix up letters and numbers. "I was so excited, I guess I didn't pay attention," I said. I scratched Max's ears. "We better go to bed before we wake up Mom and Dad. A grumpy mom plus a grumpy dad—" *Oh no!*

"No, Max!" said Connor.

But it was too late. Max heard the cue word. He started barking and barking and barking. His tail was wagging so hard, his rear end was swinging back and forth.

Connor tried winking. "Max! Max! Look at me!" He winked and winked and winked, but Max was too happy, and he liked barking too much. I tried dancing, but it didn't make Max stop. He just danced with me.

We heard a bedroom door open. It banged against the wall.

Uh-oh.

Chapter Two

Mom and Dad ran into the living room. Mom's hair stuck out in a bunch of different places, and Dad had a baseball bat in his hand. Max yelped and stopped barking. He hid behind me.

Halmoni—that's Korean for "grandmother"—came out of her bedroom. Max ran to her, and she scratched his head.

"What's going on?" asked Mom.

Dad swung his bat. "Is it a burglar? Was that why Max was barking?"

"No, I'm sorry," I said. "I mixed up the numbers on the clock because I was excited to practice with Max."

"Oh." Dad put down the bat. "Max was barking a lot. What was the math question?"

"I asked Connor what would happen if you added a grumpy mom and a grumpy dad together," I said.

"That's easy," said Halmoni. "You'd get an early bedtime for both of them." She turned to Mom and Dad. "Go back to bed."

"I'm not tired anymore," said Dad.

"Yes you are. Go to bed," said Halmoni.

"I don't want to go to bed," said Mom.

"Go to bed," said Halmoni.

"Aw, Mom." Dad dropped his bat. "But I'm not tired!"

"No more arguing." Halmoni sent Mom and Dad back to bed.

"Isn't that amazing?" I whispered to Connor. "She can make the grown-ups do anything."

"When I grow up, I want to be a halmoni," said Connor. "Then I'll make Mom and Dad give me a later bedtime."

"You'll make a great halmoni," I said.

Connor grinned.

Aren't I such a great, wonderful big sister?

Halmoni turned to us. "How about if we sit quietly for a little while and read? I'd like to look through the books for a costume for Max. Or you can go back to sleep too."

Connor and I looked at each other.

"Books," I said.

"Definitely books," said Connor.

We had been reading a lot lately because it had been raining a lot. We had read about wind and clouds and rain and lightning storms.

Connor picked up a book and showed me the cover. "Can you guess where the largest desert on Earth is?"

"That's easy," I said. "Africa. It's the Sahara Desert."

He shook his head. "Nope. It's Antarctica."

"What? No!"

He opened the book and showed me the page. "See? The Sahara Desert is about 3.5 million square miles, but Antarctica is 5 million square miles."

That was a lot of miles! Connor and I sat on the couch and read. After a while we went to help Halmoni look for a costume for Max.

"This one." Connor showed us the picture. "If Max is going to do math, we should dress him up as a professor for the costume part of the contest."

"Hmm." Halmoni took the book. "There are a lot of items here—a pipe and a vest and a coat. Max doesn't like it when we put too many things on him."

"Maybe we should check with Babu," said Connor.

Babu is Swahili for *grandfather*. He's Mom's dad, and he is very clever. "That's a good idea," I said.

Halmoni agreed. "I'll send him an email. Now how about if we make some breakfast? Who wants some muffins with oranges, white chocolate and oatmeal in them?"

Delicious! We put away the books. Connor and I helped Halmoni make breakfast. Then came my favorite part—eating! I had four muffins. They were buttery and sweet. After we cleaned up, we went to the computer to email Babu and see if there were any new cases for us.

This summer had been the bestest. Connor and I had become private investigators, or PIs. We had solved the mystery of Mrs. Robinson's lost key to the library, and we had found out who had stolen a pair of diamond earrings from the general store. We'd discovered who had been playing pranks on the theater company and who had destroyed a contestant's entry for a bake-off. It had been a busy summer, but I was always up for more mysteries.

Halmoni signed into the computer and opened up her email. "My goodness," she said and put on her glasses. "Look at this! Connor and Lark, you have a request for some sleuthing help." She ~~peared pieered~~ peered at the screen. "Oh my, this request is quite mysterious."

Connor and I stood on either side of her as she read the message aloud.

"*Dear Lark and Connor Sheep, I have a mysterious case for you. But I can't talk about it here. Please come to my house, and I will tell you everything. Sincerely, Sophie McCallister.*"

Sophie had a case for us? This was so exciting! Sophie is my best friend, but she doesn't know it yet.

Connor made a frowny face. "I don't mind helping Sophie, but I wish she'd stop calling us sheep."

"If she bugs you, I can take the case myself," I said.

Connor shook his head. "No, you and I are a team, but I think she's being mean."

"She is being funny, not mean. It's—" I couldn't think of the word, but it was a great one.

It started with a *d* or an *n*, and it meant being super sure about something. "I'm positive."

"Well, if you're both up for the case, let's get this show on the road," said Halmoni. "Just let me finish going through my email."

Connor stepped close to me. "I think Halmoni's mixed up about something. We're practicing for the pet show. We're not traveling with Max. We're just going to talk to Sophie."

I nodded. "Plus, roads are dangerous. We should never take anything on them, especially Max."

I decided to talk to Halmoni about the danger of roads later. Right now, there was a mystery to solve!

Chapter Three

Halmoni decided to stay home to give Max a bath. I packed my notebook. Then Connor and I walked to Sophie's house. The rain had stopped, and the sun was out. It was still windy though. Everything was warm and bright. The air smelled sweet and fresh. On the way to Sophie's, we spotted Mr. Ian. He was the head judge for the pet show. Mr. Ian saw us and started to walk over.

"He looks frazzled," I said to Connor.

"Raspberries?" Connor looked around. "I don't see any."

"No," I said. "Frazzled."

"Freckles?" he asked.

"Mr. Ian looks frazzled!" I yelled.

"Oh, sorry!" Connor pressed his fingers to his ear. "It's hard to hear you above the wind."

"It's okay!" I yelled so he could hear me. But the wind had stopped for a minute, so I ended up just yelling at him.

"Stop yelling! I can hear you!" he said. Then Connor frowned. "Wait. What's *frazzled*? It rhymes with *dazzled*. Is Mr. Ian sparkling or bright?"

"No, it means you're tired and stressed out at the same time."

Connor nodded. "He does look frazzled. His hair is all messy."

It was true. Mr. Ian's curly hair stuck out at a bunch of angles, his shirt was rumpled, and his shoelaces were untied. Worst of all, he looked like he was trying not to cry.

"I'm so glad I found you," Mr. Ian said as he came up to us. "I need your help. The pet show is a disaster!"

"What happened?" asked Connor.

"What *hasn't* happened?" he moaned. "We have a new moving crew, and they lost a bunch of our boxes. The pavilion for the band took longer to build than it was supposed to. This morning Mr. Rupert accused Miss Ruby of stealing his ferret, but she says he's hiding her dog. Now I have two contestants fighting. Even worse, there really *are* missing pets!"

Missing animals? I shivered. I hated to think of them lost or scared. "That's extra terrible," I said. "Missing pets are a sad thing."

"We know Aerie and Hellie," said Connor. "The library has Paws for Reading every Tuesday night. That's when people can bring their pets and you can read to the animals. Halmoni and our parents bring Max. Aerie and Hellie come every week with Miss Ruby and Mr. Rupert."

I nodded. "The pets love reading with everyone."

"Hellie and Aerie both love the soft cushions and quiet corners. They like being together and having people read to them," said Connor. He blinked fast. "This is horrible. I hate thinking about them being away from their families."

"It makes me feel terrible too." Mr. Ian nodded glumly. "I need some help. I know you

solved a lot of cases this summer. Please, could you help me?"

I nodded. "Yes."

Connor's face went all worried. "Helping to find missing pets is a big deal. But we're supposed to be helping Sophie."

Crickets! "You're right," I said to him.

Mr. Ian wrung his hands. "You can't help?"

"Sure we can," said Connor. "There's two of us and two cases." He turned to me. The wind was back, and it blew his hair straight up. "We can each take one."

"Where should we run?" I asked.

"We should each take one," he repeated.

"What about the sun?" I asked.

"We should each take one!" he yelled over the howling wind. "You take a case, and I'll take a case!"

"That's good thinking," I said as the wind quieted down. "You're a very clever little brother."

He sighed. "Twins, Lark. We're twins."

I knew he'd say that, because I'm a very good big sister, but I didn't tell him that.

"Which case do you want?" he asked.

"I should go to Sophie," I said. "She annoys you, but she's my best friend."

"You're right," he said. "She does annoy me, which is why I should help her. I should try to like her, like you do."

"Are you sure?" I asked.

He nodded. "It would be nice if we could all be friends."

I turned to Mr. Ian. "May I please use your phone to call home? Halmoni gave us permission to go to Sophie's house. I need to make sure it's okay for us to change our plans."

"Of course," he said and handed me his phone.

I talked to Halmoni, then Connor talked to Halmoni, and then Mr. Ian talked to Halmoni. Once everything was sorted, Connor gave me a high five and left for Sophie's house.

"Okay." I turned to Mr. Ian. "Let's go to the show."

He smiled. "Thank you, Lark. I'm so relieved."

This was exciting *and* scary. Connor and I had two cases in one day, which was exciting. But we were also working by ourselves, which was scary. My heart thumped in my chest. I hoped I could help Mr. Ian. The pet show had been held at the park every year since Connor and I were babies. There was an ~~agleity~~, ~~ajillety~~, agility course, a costume contest and the talent show.

Everyone loved the chance to meet other people's animals and see the neat things they could do. Plus, it was a chance to learn interesting things about the different animals. Mr. Rupert had taught us that ferrets used to help farmers protect their grain from rodents. Miss Ruby had taught us that dogs can use their amazing sense of smell to help doctors diagnose cancer.

Mr. Ian walked toward the park. I took a breath and followed him. I really hoped today was going to be the bestest day ever.

Chapter Four

When Mr. Ian and I got to the park, we spotted Miss Ruby and Mr. Rupert inside the yellow and red event tent. They were facing each other. It was easy to see them. And hear them.

The table with the kennels stood between them. Mr. Rupert and Miss Ruby were screaming at each other. Miss Ruby's face was all scrunchy and mad. Even her pink hair looked angry. Mr. Rupert's bow tie was untied, and his face was bright red.

"Wow," I said. "They're very angry."

Mr. Ian sighed. "Sometimes it's hard for grown-ups to remember to use their polite voices." He put his hand on my shoulder. "Let's see what we can do."

We went over to the arguing adults, and Mr. Ian said, "Lark is here to help."

But they didn't hear Mr. Ian because they were too busy yelling at each other.

Mr. Ian put his fingers to his mouth and whistled.

It was loud and high-pitched, and it made my ears ring.

The grown-ups stopped yelling.

"That's better," said Mr. Ian. "Lark has agreed to help us." He gave each of them a stern look. "I'm sure we all agree that in times like these, more help is welcome. And I'm sure we'll be excellent

role models and show Lark how we can work together to solve problems."

Mr. Rupert and Miss Ruby glared at each other. Then they turned to me, and both of them talked at once. It was very confusing and very loud.

"Calm down!" Mr. Ian waved his hands. "And use your polite voices." He glared at the adults. "Lark is here to help."

Miss Ruby pressed her hands to her face. "I'll take all the help I can get," she whispered. "I'm so worried."

"Me too," said Mr. Rupert. "We'll work with Lark." He glanced at Miss Ruby. "And we'll be polite about it."

"I will leave you to sort through this," Mr. Ian said to me as he walked away.

"Let me tell you what happened first, Lark," said Mr. Rupert. "After all, my Hellie is a three-time champion at the pet show."

Miss Ruby stepped in front of him. "I should be the first to talk. My Aerie needs help." She glared at Mr. Rupert. "And she is also a three-time champion. She's an excellent dog."

"Both of your friends are missing," I said. "That means they need equal help."

"That's true." Miss Ruby turned to Mr. Rupert. "You can go first."

"It happened this morning," Mr. Rupert said. "I came to set up Hellie's space. *She* was already here." He pointed at Miss Ruby. "I set Hellie next to Aerie. Miss Ruby and I talked for a moment, and then I went to get something to eat."

Sometimes being a PI means asking tough questions, and this was one of those times. "Did you talk to each other or did you argue?" I asked.

Miss Ruby blushed. "Argued," she said. "We may have raised our voices and pounded on the tables," she added, looking away.

Mr. Rupert coughed. "Yes, well, never mind that."

Time for another tough question. I turned to Miss Ruby. "If you and Mr. Rupert were fighting, why did you put Hellie's and Aerie's kennels beside each other?" I asked.

"Oh, Aerie and Hellie love each other," said Miss Ruby. "They're happiest when they're together."

Having the kennels next to each other made sense. The pets were very good friends.

Hellie liked to ride on Aerie's back. I wished Mr. Rupert and Miss Ruby could be friends instead of yelling at each other. "What happened after your argument?" I asked Mr. Rupert.

"After I had my breakfast, I came back to feed Hellie and found his kennel was empty," he said. He glared at Miss Ruby. "And we all know who unlocked his kennel."

"It wasn't me!" Miss Ruby pointed at him. "You're the one who took Aerie. Where are you hiding her?"

"You took my Hellie, and I can prove it." He slapped his hands on his jacket pockets. "I just had it—it's a pencil. It's your pencil. I found it beside Hellie's kennel. It's proof you were there."

"Your kennel is so old and beat-up. Maybe Hellie opened it and ran away because he didn't want to be in there anymore," Miss Ruby said.

I gasped. Halmoni, Mom and Dad would never let Connor and I say such mean things to anyone!

"Mr. Rupert is behind my dog's disappearance, and I can prove it," said Miss Ruby. "I found ferret hairs inside Aerie's kennel. I bet they fell off his clothes when he reached in and took my dog."

"It's animal hair," sneered Mr. Rupert. "The wind probably blew it in there."

Before they could start fighting again, I asked, "Why do you each think the other person took your pet?"

"This year the pet show has a new category called Pet of the Day," said Miss Ruby. "Every pet is up for the award. It's obvious that Mr. Rupert took Aerie so Hellie would win."

"That's not true!" said Mr. Rupert. "She took Hellie so Aerie would win!"

Crickets. Their fighting was going to give me a headache.

"I can try to help!" I yelled so they would hear me over their fighting and the wind. "But I need some information." I wished Connor was here.

He's faster at taking notes. Plus, his printing is ~~neeter kneeter~~ neater than mine. But shhh...don't tell him I said that.

"Mr. Rupert, if I give you my notebook, will you please write down what everyone says?" I asked. "We have two missing friends, and it takes me a long time to print. The faster we get the clues, the better."

Mr. Rupert took my notebook and said, "I'm happy to help. Anything to get my boy back."

"Get Mr. Rupert's statements on record so there's proof he took my dog," said Miss Ruby.

"More like get *your* words on record to prove your guilt," said Mr. Rupert.

"You took my dog because you knew she'd win the award."

Mr. Rupert's face went red. "Hellie is going to win. He's a champion."

"Your ferret doesn't do anything but sit there. Aerie can do tricks!"

"My ferret is amazing at dress-up. He's got an auto mechanic costume and a feather boa for when he pretends he's a singer—"

"But my Aerie can *actually* sing," said Miss Ruby.

"Maybe we should talk one on one," I suggested. I read that in a book I once borrowed. The detective in the story separated the people in the case because they kept arguing with each other. I bet the detective did it because all the yelling gave him a headache.

Both Miss Ruby and Mr. Rupert shook their heads.

"No," said Miss Ruby. "I want to hear everything he says."

"Me too," said Mr. Rupert. "I want to make sure she doesn't lie."

I sighed. Grown-ups can be a lot of work.

It took a long time to get all the information because Miss Ruby and Mr. Rupert kept interrupting each other. I asked them when they had last seen their pets and what they had last done with their pets. I also asked if they had seen anyone else beside their pets' kennels.

"I only saw him." Miss Ruby pointed at Mr. Rupert. "That's why I know he did it."

"Liar! You did it!" yelled Mr. Rupert.

"We should put up Lost signs for your pets," I said.

"Already done," said Miss Ruby, "and we're each offering a reward."

After I had finished asking my questions, I went to find a quiet spot. I rubbed my aching stomach. I wished again that Connor was with me, but he was helping Sophie. I took out my notebook and checked Mr. Rupert's notes.

SATURDAY MORNING

8:00 AM —

- *Mr. Rupert and Miss Ruby get into an argument over whose pet will win the Pet of the Day Prize.*
- *Mr. Rupert said Hellie will win because he's a champion.*
- *Miss Ruby said Aerie will win because Hellie doesn't know any tricks but Aerie does.*

8:10 AM —

- *Both of them leave to get breakfast for themselves and their pets.*

8:15 AM —

- Mr. Rupert comes back and finds Hellie's kennel is empty. He also finds a pencil beside the kennel.

8:16 AM —

- Miss Ruby comes back and finds Aerie is missing. She also finds ferret fur in Aerie's kennel.

Hmm, that wasn't much to go on. I went to the pet tent and checked the two kennels. The doors were open, but none of the wires were bent. That meant no one had broken into the kennels to get Aerie and Hellie. This was double and triple not much to go on. I closed my notebook and put it in my bag.

I decided to go and find Connor. Maybe he was having better luck. I hoped so. If he had already solved Sophie's mystery, he could help me with mine.

Chapter Five

Sophie's house backed onto the park. I went to her back gate and tried to open it, but it was stuck. So I took the longer ~~root rote~~ route. I walked in the sunshine and wind and tried to figure out who would unlock the animal kennels. I couldn't imagine anyone doing it, and I doubly couldn't imagine Mr. Rupert or Miss Ruby doing something like that. Taking someone's pet was...I couldn't think of the word, but it meant "really, really, terribly awful."

It was a good word, and I think it began with a d or an *s*.

I got so caught up in my thinking and imagining and wondering, I didn't look at where I was going. As I turned toward Sophie's house, I tripped on the sidewalk and fell on the grass. ~~Lukily Lookely~~ Luckily I didn't hurt myself.

"Lark Ba, that's an odd place to sit."

I looked up and saw Sophie's mom. "Hello, Mrs. McCallister. I tripped."

"You shouldn't do that," she said. "That's how kids get hurt."

I stood up. "I was just going to see Sophie and Connor. Are they still at your house?"

"Hmm," said Mrs. McCallister. "I'm not sure. Sophie went to the bird people this morning. I'm not sure where she is now or if Connor is with her."

"Bird people? Do you mean the aviary?"

"No, no," said Mrs. McCallister. "The bird people." She made a face. "Goodness, why can't I remember their names?"

"Oh." I stopped and thought like Sophie and Mrs. McCallister. "Do you mean Mr. and Mrs. Sparrow?"

"Yes! That's it! Thank you, Lark. The Sparrows. But Sophie might be back home again. I'm glad you and Connor are going to spend time with her. Something is upsetting her, but she won't tell me what it is."

"Do you remember when she first got upset?"

Mrs. McCallister tapped her chin. "Six days ago, after the rain started. She wouldn't go into the basement to play. Then later she wouldn't go up to the attic to read. At first I thought she was upset because we've been having renovations done to the house. We need to replace our roof,

44

and we need a new fence and new windows. The house is old, and all those things have warped over time."

I frowned. "Warped?"

"As houses get older, it's harder for them to deal with the weather," said Mrs. McCallister. "When it rains or snows, the moisture makes the wood expand and bend."

I snapped my fingers. "That's why I couldn't open your back gate!"

She nodded. "Yes, but once the fence is replaced, you won't have any problems." She looked toward her house. "But the renovations have been loud and dirty. Sometimes it's been hard to find time for Sophie because I'm so busy with the construction people. Sophie said she didn't mind, but I think she's scared of something. And being scared...that's not like Sophie."

"Okay, thank you. I'll go see if she's home."

I jogged to Sophie's house. Mrs. McCallister was right. Sophie was very brave. I wondered what had scared her. When I got closer, I saw Connor and Sophie sitting on the front steps, and I did not like what I saw. Nope, nope, nope. My brother and my friend were glaring at each other.

"Baa, Baa, Lark Sheep," said Sophie. "Thank goodness you're here."

"Argh," said Connor. "I don't like you calling us sheep."

Sophie scowled. "I'm not calling *you* Connor Sheep because you said you didn't like it. I'm calling *Lark* Lark Sheep, and she doesn't mind."

"It's true," I said. "I think it's funny because our last name is Ba, and that's the sound sheep make."

Connor sighed. "As you can see, Sophie and I didn't get very far in our investigation."

"Yes we did," said Sophie. "We learned you don't like being called Connor Sheep."

"That's true," he said, "but I mean we didn't get very far in solving your mystery."

"I didn't get very far in mine either," I said, and I told them what had happened.

"Grown-ups who argue are the worst," said Sophie. "Your mystery is more important than mine, Lark. We have to find the missing pets before it gets dark. They may not have eaten for a while, and I bet they're scared." She turned to Connor. "We can wait for mine to be solved."

Connor blinked. "That's nice of you, but you asked for help. Plus, there's two of us, so we can do both cases."

"There's three of us," said Sophie. "Maybe if we all work on Lark's case, it will help. Three heads are better than one."

Connor frowned. "I think it's hard enough to have one head."

"No, *three heads are better than one* means that if we work as a team, things will get done," I said.

"Oh," said Connor. "That makes more sense."

She folded her arms. "I want to find Aerie and Hellie because I like them a lot, and they need all the help they can get."

It was nice to have a friend like Sophie. "What is your mystery about?" I asked Sophie.

She shivered. "I think our house is haunted."

Her words made *me* shiver. "Haunted?"

Sophie nodded. "There have been strange noises. I think the ghost is howling." She crossed her arms across her chest. "Maybe they're crying. Do you think they're mad at us for being in their house?"

"What do ghosts sound like?" asked Connor.

"It's a cross between a wail and a siren," said Sophie. She closed her eyes and imitated them. "*Oooowwwwwwooooo! Oooowwwwwwooooo!*"

"That almost sounds like a dog howling," said Connor.

Wait. Wait! Strange noises? Howling? Aerie and Hellie were missing. The park was on the other side of Sophie's backyard. Maybe this was where the pets were! Maybe they were in her house and making noises! "When did this happen? Did it start today?" I took out my notebook and handed it to my brother.

Connor handed it back. "I already have the notes. It started last week."

My shoulders slumped. So much for solving my case by finding Aerie and Hellie at Sophie's house. "Okay, tell me everything."

Sophie nodded. "There have been weird shadows on the wall and strange sounds. But when I went and looked outside, there was nothing there but the trees and lawn." She rubbed her arms. "A few times last week—at least three times—I found the front door open even though I'd seen Mom close it. My parents are fixing up the house, and there has been all kinds of noise from people walking on the roof or the wind rushing through the vents. The construction people finished for the morning, but the sounds are getting worse. Louder and different. This morning I ran outside and looked around when I heard them, but there wasn't anything there."

I shuddered. That *was* creepy.

"And now the noises are everywhere. Inside and outside the house," said Sophie. "Scratching and howling ghost sounds. I think something came into the house. I think we have a rain ghost. Mom keeps asking what's bugging me, but I can't tell her until we have proof."

"I don't know about proof of a rain ghost," said Connor, "but there are definitely weird noises in the house. I heard them too."

"I wonder why the ghost would haunt you now. It's never bothered you before."

"It's the rain and the wind," said Sophie. "I think they blew the ghost here."

"But you heard the ghost today?" I asked.

She nodded.

"Why would the ghost still be here if it's sunny?" Connor made a frowny face. "It's not raining anymore, so why doesn't it leave?"

"I think it's trapped," said Sophie. "The mystery is how to find it and set it free. We can do that after we find Aerie and Hellie."

"We should go back to the park and take another look at the kennels in the tent," I said. "There might be a clue I missed."

"Then we should go to the library," said Connor. "I bet they have books on ghost hunting and pet finding."

"That's a good idea," I said. "Let's go." I smiled at Connor. He might be my little brother, but he really is a great big help, and I was glad we were a team again.

Chapter Six

Mr. Ian had strung a rope around Aerie's and Hellie's kennels and locked them so no one would touch them. We crawled underneath the tables and looked around.

"Mr. Rupert said he found Miss Ruby's pencil beside Hellie's kennel," I said, "and Miss Ruby said she found ferret fur in Aerie's kennel, but that might have been because of the wind and rain."

"There is a lot of trampled grass," said Connor. "That's too bad—we can't look for tracks."

"What about fingerprints?" asked Sophie. "When my babushka—my grandma—and I watch mystery shows, the detectives always take fingerprints."

"That's a good idea," I said, "but there are too many people around. Anyone could have touched the kennels."

"Being an investigator is much harder than it seems," said Sophie. "What if I walk around the park and look for the pets?"

"That's a good idea," I said.

"I'll ask around too," she said. "Maybe someone spotted them. Oh, look! There's Franklin and Kate."

They are our other friends. I waved to them, and they waved back. "Maybe they can help," I said. "The more people looking, the better."

"I'm going to start searching for the pets," said Sophie. "Good luck, Lark Sheep and Connor Ba, not a sheep. We'll meet back here later."

Connor shook his head and sighed. "Good luck to you too."

After she had left, he said, "Do you think Mr. Rupert took Aerie and then hid Hellie so he wouldn't be a suspect? Or that maybe Miss Ruby did the same thing, except she took Hellie and hid Aerie?"

"I don't know," I said. "I hope not. Stealing pets from their families is mean. Neither Mr. Rupert nor Miss Ruby is a mean person. Hellie and Aerie probably got lost. Now they're scared, and they've missed breakfast."

"Lark and Connor!" Halmoni walked toward us with Max on the leash. "How is it going?"

"Not so great," I said. I bent down and scratched Max's ears. "But Max looks fantastic."

"Thank you," said Halmoni. "I thought about what Connor suggested for Max's costume.

Putting a bow tie on Max's collar makes him look like a professor, and Max doesn't mind wearing his collar, so it is a good compromise." She straightened his tie. "Tell me more about the mysteries."

Connor told her about the rain ghost, and I told her about the missing pets.

"We looked for clues in the kennels, but we didn't see anything." I looked at Max. "But Max might be able to help." I took out the blanket from Aerie's kennel. "Max, smell this. Can you find Aerie?"

"Good thinking," said Connor. "Max is a great tracker!"

Max sniffed the blanket, then sniffed the ground and started walking. We followed and followed, but after ten minutes Halmoni said, "I think there are too many scents for Max to follow."

I bent down and gave him a tummy rub.

So did Connor. "You tried your best, and you did really great, Max."

Max's tail thumped in ~~appresciastion~~ ~~appearciatshun~~ appreciation.

"Connor and I thought we'd go to the library and look for some help in the books." I stood up.

"That's a great idea," said Halmoni. "Way to use your noodle."

Connor stood up and whispered, "Is she talking about a pool noodle? Because we don't have one."

"I don't know," I whispered back. "We'll have to ask her later. Now it's time to solve the mysteries."

We went to the library and told Mrs. Robinson, the librarian, about our cases.

"Those are two interesting mysteries," said Mrs. Robinson. "Let's see what we can find."

We followed Mrs. Robinson through the library aisles. ~~They're their~~ There were so many amazing books, but now wasn't the time to look at them. We had two cases to solve.

Mrs. Robinson pulled a book off the shelf and flipped through it. "There isn't a lot of information on ghosts," she said, "but this book is a history of the town. If there were any hauntings in Sophie's house, it would be in here."

We sat together and read the pages, but they weren't helpful. Mrs. Robinson sighed as she closed the last book. "I'm afraid there's no record of any ghosts living near Sophie's house."

"Thanks for your help," I said to Mrs. Robinson. "We'll keep searching."

"The animal section is over there." She pointed. "You might find some useful tips for finding lost pets."

We went and searched through the books. "This book says we should put up Lost Pet signs and offer a reward," said Connor.

"Mr. Ian already did that," I said.

Halmoni sighed. "It's not easy to find a lost pet. The bigger the pet, the farther they can wander. The smaller the pet, the more places they can hide." She rubbed Max's head. "That's why you're always on a leash, little one."

Max wagged his tail.

We went back to the park. Franklin, Kate and Sophie found us. Together we looked in all the tiny places around Hellie's kennel, in case he had sneaked inside one of them.

Mr. Ian, Miss Ruby and Mr. Rupert came toward us.

"How is it going?" asked Mr. Ian.

"The pet show is starting in an hour," said Mr. Rupert. "Where is Hellie?"

"And Aerie," said Miss Ruby.

"We're working as hard as we can—" I began.

Miss Ruby burst into tears. "My Aerie! I'm so scared for him!"

My stomach felt wibbly. Not only were we about to lose this case, but we still hadn't figured out the haunting at Sophie's house. There were two missing pets, which made me feel awful, and we didn't have any clues. If I wasn't careful, this day was going to be my worst day ever.

Chapter Seven

"Don't be discouraged," said Halmoni. "I know if you put your heads together, you'll figure it out."

"Kate and I can keep looking around the park for Hellie and Aerie," said Franklin.

"Max and I will come along," said Halmoni. She hugged Connor, Sophie and me. "I know you will try your best."

They left.

"When you were on the case of the lost key, we acted out the moment the key went missing," said Sophie. "Maybe we could act out Miss Ruby and Mr. Rupert fighting—it might help. Come on. Let's try this so I can fight with Connor!"

"I don't know if that will help," said Connor. "And I don't want you yelling at me."

Sophie smiled. "But you get to yell at me too, Connor Wool."

Connor frowned. "Connor Wool?"

"Because sheep make wool, and wool is warm and cozy, just like you."

Connor grinned. "Okay. Let's go fight like grown-ups!"

We took our spots around the table. I made sure the kennels sat in the center of the tables. Then I told everyone all I remembered about how Mr. Rupert and Miss Ruby had yelled at each other and banged their fists.

"My pet is better than yours!" yelled Sophie.

"Is not!" Connor yelled back. "My dog can sit and stay. Your ferret can't do any of that!"

They were really good at fighting. They yelled and stomped and slammed their hands on the table.

"I'm going to get my ferret food," huffed Sophie. She stormed off. Then she ran back. "Oops, I forgot the bowl."

"What are you children doing?" Mr. Ian asked. He walked toward us with Miss Ruby and Mr. Rupert.

"Sophie and Connor are pretending to be Miss Ruby and Mr. Rupert. They are going over what happened when Aerie and Hellie went missing," I said.

"I was at the spot where I get the bowl for my ferret food," said Sophie as she reached for the bowl. Her hand froze in midair, and her eyes went wide.

Connor and I looked at what she was looking at.

"We know who opened the doors!" we all yelled at the same time.

Chapter Eight

"It was Mr. Rupert and Miss Ruby," I said.

"They stole each other's animals?" asked Mr. Ian. "That's terrible!"

"I never stole Aerie," said Mr. Rupert. He glared at me.

"And I didn't steal Hellie," said Miss Ruby. She glared at Connor.

"You didn't steal them," said Connor. "You accidentally let them go." He pointed at the kennels. "Lark said when you argued, you hit the table. When Sophie and I pretended to be you, we hit the table too. Look! All the hitting made the doors open."

They looked at the kennels. Miss Ruby put her hand to her mouth. "Oh no. No!"

"You were so busy arguing, you didn't notice," I said. "Miss Ruby, you said Hellie's kennel is old, so the lock was probably loose."

"And Mrs. Robinson said that when it rains, stuff can get warped," added Connor. "So maybe Aerie's lock wasn't locking properly."

"And when you went to get their breakfast, they snuck out," I said.

Mr. Rupert started to cry. "I didn't mean to do it."

"I just wanted Aerie to win so everyone could see how amazing she is." Miss Ruby was crying too.

"Aerie and Hellie are *both* amazing," said
Sophie. "They don't need a prize to prove it."

"Do you know where they are?" asked Mr. Ian.

I felt terrible. This was the worst kind of feeling. I knew how the pets had gotten out, but I didn't know where they were.

"Not yet," I said. That made Mr. Rupert and Miss Ruby cry louder.

"Maybe I'll take the adults over here," Mr. Ian said, leaning close to me and Connor. "See what you can do, okay?"

I nodded.

"What now?" asked Sophie.

I wasn't sure. My bestest day had become my worstest day.

Chapter Nine

I wanted to cry, but Sophie said, "It's okay, Lark. We can figure this out together."

Connor nodded. "Three heads are better than one."

I took a deep breath and closed my eyes.

"It's too bad there wasn't a bad guy in this mystery," said Sophie. "In the mysteries my babushka and I watch, the cops always catch the bad guys by figuring out why they committed the crime—they call it a motive."

My eyes snapped open. "Sophie, you're right! But it's not just bad guys who have a reason for doing things. All of us have reasons for doing stuff. Maybe Hellie and Aerie had a reason for leaving their kennels."

Connor snapped his fingers. "Mr. Rupert and Miss Ruby were yelling at each other because each one wanted their pet to win."

"Aerie and Hellie hate loud noises," said Sophie. "Whenever we read together in the library, they like soft voices and quiet spaces!"

"Exactly!" I hugged myself, and then I hugged Connor and Sophie. "They wanted a quiet place."

"Where would they go?" Sophie spun in a circle. "Not to the park. That's too loud. They'd go this way." She pointed to the left. "It's quieter."

"Come on!"

We spread out and ran. We called and called
for them.

The wind was blowing hard, and then it
started to rain. We yelled louder.

Sophie ran over to me. Connor joined us.

"Why are you yelling for Ronald?" Sophie asked.

"I'm not. I'm yelling 'Aerie' and 'Hellie,'" I said.

Connor made a growly sound. "It's the wind. It's changing the sounds."

"So they don't know we're calling for them?" Sophie asked sadly. She swiped at her eyes. "This is terrible!"

"We'll find them," I said. "We're not giving up."

She pointed across the street. "We're close to my house. Let's go and get some raincoats so we can keep looking."

Connor froze. "Wait a second. Sophie, you said the noises got worse today."

"They did."

"What did the noises *use* to sound like?" he asked.

Sophie closed her eyes. "*Oooowwwwwwooooo! Oooowwwwwwooooo!*"

"And now?" I asked.

"*Aaaoooooo, skritch, skritch. Aaaoooooow-waaaooo, skritch, skritch.*"

Connor and I looked at each other.

"Sophie," he said. "You went outside this morning to investigate the noise. What time was that?"

She shrugged. "Maybe a little after eight?"

"Oh my gosh, Sophie," I said. "We have to get to your house!"

"What's going on?" She checked the road to make sure it was clear, then waved for us to cross.

"It's the noises!" I said.

"And the wind!" added Connor.

We ran into her house.

"Where is the quietest place in your house?"
I asked.

"The attic! Come on!" Sophie ran up the stairs
two at a time. She threw open the door.

Aerie was curled up on the other side. Hellie
was on her back.

"We found them!" I cheered. "We found them!"

Chapter Ten

"I'm confused." Miss Ruby held Aerie close. "How did you know they were at Sophie's house?"

We were back at the park. Hellie and Aerie were being cuddled by their human parents.

"It's like this," I said. "Hellie and Aerie ran from their kennels because you were yelling and pounding on the tables."

Mr. Rupert blushed. "I'm sorry, Miss Ruby. I behaved badly."

"Me too," she said. "Both of our pets are amazing. We shouldn't have been fighting."

"Aerie and Hellie don't like noise," said Sophie. "They ran away. They wouldn't have gone to the park because that's loud too." She looked at Connor. "Then what happened?"

"Three things," said Connor. "The construction people were leaving your house, so your door was open. You went outside to investigate the noise."

"Your mom said you're replacing a bunch of things because the weather makes stuff warp, like windows and fences. I bet the same thing happened to your doors. Remember?" I said to Sophie. "You said your mom had closed the doors, but you kept finding them open. I think the rain meant the doors weren't locking properly. Just like with the kennels."

"Aerie and Hellie must have seen me when I went outside," said Sophie. "They followed me in and went for the quietest spot in the house. Because it had stopped raining, they didn't leave any pawprints in the house."

"The door must have closed on them," said Halmoni.

"The wind's been making everything sound weird," said Connor. "When Aerie was calling and Hellie was scratching, it sounded like a ghost."

"I'm so glad everyone is safe and back home," said Halmoni. She looked at me. "Are you okay? You solved the case, but you don't seem very happy."

"I am happy," I said, "but I feel bad. When I was at Sophie's house earlier, I thought maybe Aerie and Hellie were there, and they were. If I had asked better questions, we could have found them much sooner."

Halmoni hugged me tightly. "You can't always know the questions you should ask. You tried your best, Lark, and that's all that matters. Aerie and Hellie are home, thanks to the hard work of the three of you. And you know what else? I'm proud of you, and I hope you're proud of you too."

I thought about it. "Yes, I am proud of me."

She hugged me again. "Good!"

Mr. Ian clapped his hands. "Let's get to the pet show."

"Aerie and I have had enough excitement for one day," said Miss Ruby. "I need some time to think about why I said such terrible things to Mr. Rupert."

"Me too," he said. "Maybe I can buy you and Aerie lunch, and I can apologize."

Miss Ruby smiled. "I'd like that."

"Oh, please," said Mr. Ian. "After everything that's happened, I wish you'd stay and be part of the show."

Miss Ruby and Mr. Rupert talked with each other and agreed to stay.

"Lark, Connor and Sophie, thank you. You did really great today," Mr. Ian said.

"Come on," said Halmoni with a smile. "Let's see that remarkable trick of Max's."

We walked to the pet show. Max did amazing at his math trick. When we ran in circles for the agility course, none of us got dizzy.

At the end of the show, Mr. Ian announced the winners, and guess what? Max won for Best Trick.

"Now it's time for the Pet of the Day award," said Mr. Ian. "For reminding us all of the importance of using soft voices, listening to each other and not letting competition get in the way of friendship, the award goes to both Aerie and Hellie!"

Everyone cheered.

"Lark Sheep and Connor Wool," said Sophie, "you solved two cases in one day and helped Aerie and Hellie!"

Connor shook his head but laughed. "You helped too, Sophie Sofa!"

"Sophie Sofa?" Sophie's forehead crinkled, and then she laughed. "Because Sophie sounds like sofa. I like it!"

"That was really interesting, how the wind made things sound different," said Sophie. "Will you help me learn more about how sounds travel?"

He nodded. "Let's go to the library!"

"That's a great idea," said Halmoni, "but before we do that, how about a trip to the ice-cream parlor to celebrate?"

Max barked and wagged his tail.

Sophie and Connor cheered. I did too, because today was the best day ever!

THE WORDS LARK LOVES

CHAPTER TWO:

"She is being funny, not mean. It's—" I couldn't think of the word, but it was a great one. It started with a d or an n, and it meant being super sure about something. *"I'm positive."*

The excellent word Lark was thinking of is *undeniable*, which means to be so sure about something, there is no doubt. For example, it's undeniable that you are an amazing person!

CHAPTER FIVE:

Taking someone's pet was...I couldn't think of the word, but it meant "really, really, terribly awful." It was a good word, and it began with a d or an s.

The word Lark was thinking of is *despicable*, which means something is so terribly awful, it's horrible. For example, stealing someone's pet is despicable.

THE STUFF LARK *ALMOST* GOT RIGHT

CHAPTER TWO:

"Well, if you're both up for the case, let's get this show on the road," said Halmoni. *"Just let me finish going through my email."*

Lark and Connor didn't quite understand what Halmoni meant by this phrase. To *get the show on the road* means to get started on your project or event.

CHAPTER SIX:

"That's a great idea," said Halmoni. *"Way to use your noodle."*

Lark and Connor thought Halmoni was talking about pool noodles. But *using your noodle* is a fun way of saying someone's being clever and using their brainpower.

NATASHA DEEN loves stories: exciting ones, scary ones and, especially, funny ones! As a kid of two countries (Guyana and Canada), she feels especially lucky because she gets a double dose of stories. Natasha is the author of many books, including the Lark Ba Detective series in the Orca Echoes line, several titles in the Orca Soundings line and *In the Key of Nira Ghani*, which won the Amy Mathers Teen Book Award and was nominated for the Red Maple Award. Natasha lives in Edmonton.